Christie Plays Field Hockey

by

Susan O'Hara

Illustrated by Rebecca Barrett

Strategic Book Publishing and Rights Co.

Sweetie, I love watching you play!

Book Design/Layout by Kalpart. Visit www.kalpart.com

Strategic Book Publishing and Rights Co.
12620 FM 1960, Suite A4-507
Houston, TX 77065
www.sbpra.com

ISBN: 978-1-62857-991-8

Other books by Susan O'Hara

Tim's First Baseball Game

Tim's First Soccer Game

Christie Plays Softball

Christie wanted to play softball for her school team. She had played softball for a long time. She loved softball. She was good at softball. She had many friends who played softball, but Christie's new school didn't have a softball team. With no softball team, Christie needed to find a new sport to play.

my first
softball game

me
(christie)

my
team

The Blue Wave

During gym class, the girls tried a variety of different sports to see what they liked playing the best. There was a golf team, a tennis team, a volleyball team, and a field hockey team to try out for. Christie thought she might like to try field hockey, but she wasn't sure she knew how to play.

The teacher, Coach Ellen, showed the girls how to hold the field hockey stick and push the ball on the ground as they ran. She told them they could use only one side of the stick to hit the ball. She told them they couldn't use their feet, like in soccer, but could use only the stick to move the ball around. Then Coach Ellen said, "The goalie is the only player who can use her hands and feet to keep the ball from going into the goal."

Coach Ellen talked to Christie after class and said, "Christie, you did a really good job as goalie in field hockey during class today. Why don't you try out for the school field hockey team? I think you would be a terrific goalie."

So, the first day of field hockey practice, Christie tried out for the school field hockey team.

She put on the kickers. She put on the leg pads. She put on the chest pad. She put on the brightly colored jersey. She put on the hand guards. She put on the helmet. She held the field hockey stick in her hand. Then she stood in front of the goal.

Coach Ellen asked the girls to line up in front of the goal to take a shot with the ball and see if they could score.

The girls started shooting balls at Christie one by one.

Katie hit one ball to her right and Christie kicked it away with her foot. She saved it!

Elena hit another ball to the left. Christie ran over and kicked it away with her foot. She saved it! Neither ball went in the goal!

Becca hit the next shot and it went over Christie's head, so Christie jumped up high and hit it away with her hand.

All the girls cheered loudly! "Wow, Christie, that was great! You didn't let any balls into the net!"

Christie was excited! She had fun playing field hockey! She had fun playing goalie!

After practice was over, Christie went home.

"Mom, I made the field hockey team," she said.

Mom said, "Wow, Christie, that's great! What happened at practice?"

Christie told Mom everything that happened at field hockey practice. She said, "All the girls took shots at me in the goal and I made three saves! It was fun! Coach Ellen said I did a great job and I will be playing goalie for the team."

Christie and her team practiced hard and they were all excited for the first game.

Christie hadn't played field hockey very long. She wasn't sure she even knew all the rules of the game. She hoped she could play well.

Before the first game, she put on the kickers. She put on the leg pads. She put on the chest pad. She put on the brightly colored jersey. She put on the hand guards. She put on the helmet. She held the field hockey stick in her hand. She stood in front of the goal. Christie was excited. She was a little nervous too. She had never played in a field hockey game before!

The whistle blew to start the game. Christie's team started with the ball.

Katie got to the ball first and sent it toward Becca. Becca got the ball and passed it to Elena. Elena hit the ball toward the goal and scored!

After the goal, the referee brought the ball back to the middle of the field. The other team started with the ball. They passed the ball around, keeping it away from Christie's team. It was coming toward Christie.

Christie thought, *I can't let them score. I need to be quick and not let any balls in the net.*

The ball came closer and Christie got ready. She bent her knees and got her hands up and ready to hit the ball away. They hit it hard at the goal with their sticks. Christie had to jump up high to hit the ball so it wouldn't go in. She hit it back onto the field to Katie for her to take down to the other end of the field.

Before Katie could score, the other team got the ball back again.

They came toward Christie again. This time, they hit it off toward the side, hoping to get it past Christie. Christie dove to her left, knocking the ball out of the way. Katie ran to the ball and passed it over to Elena. Elena ran down the field pushing the ball ahead of her. She hit it to Becca. Becca shot at the goal and scored!

The rest of the game was a blur of excitement and Christie's team won 2 – 0.

Christie was excited! She had saved five balls from going into the goal. Christie and her team celebrated after the game and talked about every goal they had made and every save of the game.

When it was finally time to leave after the game, Christie found her mom and dad, gathered her equipment, and hopped in the car.

Mom said to Christie, "What is that funny stick you have in your hand?"

Christie laughed and said, "It's a lacrosse stick. The coach wants me to try out for goalie for the lacrosse team! It's time to go to practice!"

CPSIA information can be obtained
at www.ICGtesting.com
Printed in the USA
LVIC04n2341200414
382405LV00002B/4